Curious George®
Dance Party

Adaptation by Borana Greku and Alessandra Preziosi
Based on the TV series teleplay written by Raye Lankford

Houghton Mifflin Harcourt Publishing Company

Boston   New York   2013

For information about permission to reproduce selections from this book, write to Permissions, Houghton Mifflin Harcourt Publishing Company, 215 Park Avenue South, New York, New York 10003.

Library of Congress Cataloging-in-Publication Data is on file.

ISBN: 978-0-547-96819-3 paper-over-board
ISBN: 978-0-547-96820-9 paperback
ISBN: 978-0-547-96821-6 paper-over-board bilingual
ISBN: 978-0-547-96822-3 paperback bilingual

Design by Afsoon Razavi
www.hmhbooks.com
Manufactured in China
LEO 9 8 7 6 5 4 3 2 1
4500383116

AGES	GRADES	GUIDED READING LEVEL	READING RECOVERY LEVEL	LEXILE ® LE
5–7	2	J	17	370L

George was excited.
He had just received an invitation
to Allie's dance party!
He couldn't stop dancing!

He danced while he brushed
his teeth.
Sometimes he even danced
while he slept.

But George's friend Bill didn't
want to go to the party.
"I'll be the only kid who can't
dance," Bill said.

"Look," said Bill, "even the
Renkinses are practicing for
the party!"

"This is called the box step,"
said Mrs. Renkins.
George was curious. He didn't
know that dance.

Then George had an idea.
They could record the Renkinses
dancing and learn the box step!

The dance looked hard.
Bill didn't think he could learn.
"Maybe I should tell Allie I have
the chickenpox!" he said.

When they went home, George and
Bill watched the video.
"Dancing should have a map. Maps
show you where to go," Bill said.

George thought that was a great idea!
He counted the dance steps and
made a map.
Right steps were red and left steps
were blue.
He numbered them and made the
quick steps smaller than
the slow steps.

But something was still missing.
George thought about the
Renkinses.
Of course!
They needed music!

The beat of the music made dancing
much easier.
He just moved his feet to the rhythm.

The night of the party arrived.
Bill was still worried.
"I'll look silly using the map,"
he said.

George looked at the map again.
The steps were shaped like a box!
All they had to do was make a
box with their feet.

Bill danced with Mrs. Renkins.
"You dance beautifully!" she
exclaimed.

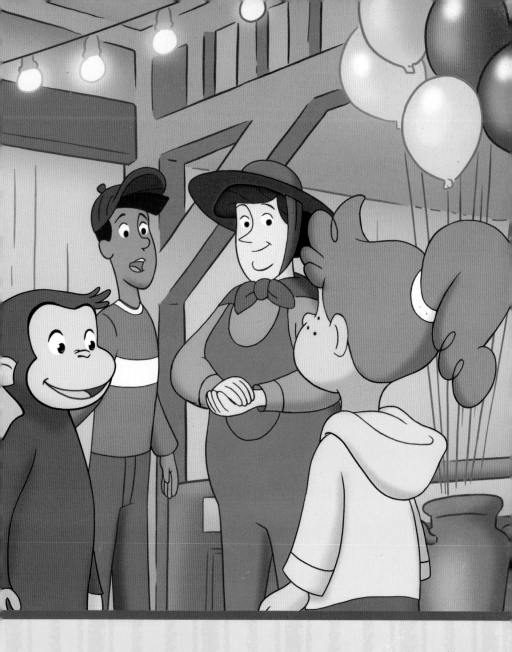

"I wish I could do that dance," Allie
said. Bill and George were surprised.
"You mean you don't know it?"
Bill asked.

"I don't know any fancy dances," Allie said.
"I just move to the music!"

Bill had been worried about dancing
for no reason!
"Could you teach that dance to the
rest of us?" Allie asked.

Allie turned on the music.
She and George were dance partners.

Bill took out the map.
He showed everyone how to do
the box step.

George and Bill danced all evening.
It was great teaching everyone the
box step, but it was even more fun
dancing with friends.

What Comes Next?

In order to dance the box step, George has to follow a certain pattern with his feet. See if you can figure out what comes next in these different patterns.

What comes next?

What comes next?

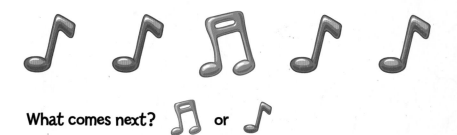

What comes next?

Make Your Own Dance Map!

You can learn the box step just like George did! All you need is a poster board, a pencil, a couple of crayons, and some feet to trace.

Create the steps

- Start with a poster board big enough to dance on. This will be your box for the box step!

- Ask an adult if you can trace their feet for the larger, slower steps. Using a pencil, trace an adult's left foot in the top left corner of the box and an adult's right foot in the bottom right corner of the box.

- Now trace your own feet for the smaller, faster steps. In the top right corner of the box, trace your left and right feet side by side. Now trace them again in the bottom left corner of the box.

- Get blue and red crayons or markers. Color all the left steps blue and the right steps red, just like George did.

Number the steps

- Start at the top left, with the big blue step. This is the first step. Write the number 1 on it.

- The second step will be red, because your feet need to take turns. Write the number 2 on the small red footprint in the top right corner, and the number 3 on the small blue step next to it.

- Write the number 4 on the big red step in the bottom right corner.

- Put a number 5 on the last blue step, and a number 6 on the last red step.

Now you're ready to use your dance map! Start at step 1 and follow the steps in order. Turn on some music and have fun dancing!

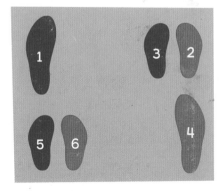